CAPPY

Dedicated to my grandchildren

They remind me every day to dream big, take risks, surmount obstacles and live a happy life. It is my hope that you and your children can have a life well-lived.

Printed in the U.S.A.

Cappy is an adorable character inspired by the author's grandson. This book creates a wonderful bonding experience between the child and the adult who share reading it. Cappy takes the readers on a magical journey of self-discovery and knowing that anything is possible.

Cappy introduces the concept of how to live a life you love living. His adventures make the principles of living such a life fun, easy and light for the reader, yet deep with meaning and learning for the audience. This story has a contagious, generous and inspiring energy that will leave one knowing the depth and wisdom in this book!

You will be so glad Cappy has come into your life.

Mary Morrissey
Speaker and Renowned Author

Cappy is very special.
He is half cat and half puppy.

Cappy was born on top of a mountain and hatched from an egg.

One of the BIGGEST puzzles about Cappy was: Is he a mammal or WHHAAAATT?!

It doesn't matter to Cappy
what he is because Cappy decided
he was going to be HAPPY!

Cappy loved running up and down hills. He loved building blocks and mazes.

And most of all
he loved Choo Choo
trains!!

Cappy had a little lisp and
every time he saw a train
he would gleefully exclaim, "Shoo Shoo!"

One day, Cappy decided that what he would really l♥ve was a set of Choo Choo trains.

Cappy could see the red Choo Choo train in his mind.

Cappy asked his mommy if she would buy one for him. His mommy loved him so much and she said, "Oh Honey, I would love to do that for you, but the train set is $300.00 and we don't have that much money."

Cappy went to sleep that night thinking how much he would love a set of Shoo Shoo trains. He started dreaming about it.

The most magical thing happened.
He saw a Fairy Godmother
just like at Disney® World.
Except, she looked like a big brain with glitters.

She was a little scary, but he decided to like her especially because she was so glittery.

In his dreams, he stared at her glitters and she whispered to him...

"Do what you can
with
what you have,"

She whispered that
over and over again.

When he woke up,
Cappy was so excited.
He did not know whether to yelp,
or purr, or bark, or meow.
"Mee Aarf!", he exclaimed.

Cappy counted up
all of his money and
found out he had
4 whole dollars.

He started thinking how he could earn $296.00 to pay for the Shoo Shoo train set he would love to have.

He was bouncing from place to place and asked his mommy if he could do some chores.

They were both so excited doing extra chores. They were singing silly songs and Cappy earned 5 whole dollars.

Oh boy, he thought this is just great!

That afternoon, Cappy and his dad went to the store. Standing in front of the store, they saw a poor kid who didn't even have shoes.

SPORTING GOODS STORE

THRIFT STORE

OPEN

Cappy's dad was a generous soul. He said to Cappy, "Let's go into this thrift store and see if we can get him some clothes."

"What's a thrift store?", Cappy asked.

Oh, it's a store where people give away things that they don't need.
The thrift store sells you those things at a very cheap price and they use that money to help other people.

Wow! Cappy thought. How amazing is that? Cappy and his dad walked through the store and found all kinds of curious things.

Then, **Cappy** spotted a nice pair of shoes he really liked. He wanted to give them to the kid with no shoes. They cost $2.00! He paid for the shoes with his own money.

He was imagining how the kid outside was going to feel about getting new shoes.

This made him smile!
And then, guess what happened??

He looked on a shelf
and there, to his wonderous
eyes, he spotted a shiny
red Shoo Shoo train set.

The best part was that they cost seven dollars!
Cappy took all the money out of his pocket,
and he had exactly $7.00. He bought the
trains that he l♥ved!

And there he went again, gleefully yelping, and purring, and barking, and meowing!! Mee Aarf!!"

That night when Cappy slept, his fairy godmother came to him again. She whispered ever so slightly: "Way to go Cappy! You noticed what you wanted, you did what you could with what you had, you even figured out how to help that little boy AND, you earned your Choo Choo trains! Well done!"

ABOUT THE AUTHOR

Dr. Lina Jarboe is a devoted wife, a mother of two and currently has eight grandchildren. She has a degree in French literature and is a highly regarded, successful dentist and root canal specialist.

Lina discovered she had dominion over the kind of life she would have. She developed her philosophy about directing her life at a very young age in a third world country.

She is an avid reader and lifelong student. Passionate about living a life fulfilled, she was inspired to write Cappy with the intention that children, along with their parents, can dream big, and have those dreams unfold into a life they love living!

Made in the USA
Columbia, SC
23 October 2020